SHERMAN CRUNCHLEY

BY LAURA NUMEROFF AND NATE EVANS
ILLUSTRATED BY TIM BOWERS

Dutton Children's Books
• NEW YORK •

E
Numeroff

FOR A LITTLE SWEETIE,
SIENA LILY RICHTER
—L.N.

001559909

FOR JESSICA AND WHITNEY—
MY DOGGONE WONDERFUL NIECES!
—N.E.

TO AMY, KYLE, JOSH, AND TYLER
—T.B.

Text copyright © 2003 by Laura Numeroff and Nate Evans
Illustrations copyright © 2003 by Tim Bowers

Library of Congress Cataloging-in-Publication Data
Numeroff, Laura Joffe.
Sherman Crunchley / by Laura Numeroff and Nate Evans; illustrated by Tim Bowers.—1st ed.
p.   cm.
Summary : Following the tradition of the Crunchley dog family,
Sherman is expected to succeed his father as Biscuit City's chief of police, but the only thing
he likes about being a police officer is the hat he wears.
ISBN 0-525-47130-8
[1. Individuality—Fiction. 2. Dogs—Fiction. 3. Police—Fiction. 4. Hats—Fiction.]
I. Evans, Nate. II. Bowers, Tim, ill. III. Title.
PZ7.N964 Sh 2003   [E]—dc21   2002040814

Published in the United States by
Dutton Children's Books
a division of Penguin Young Readers Group
345 Hudson Street, New York, New York 10014
www.penguin.com

Designed by Heather Wood
Printed in USA
First Edition
1 3 5 7 9 10 8 6 4 2

Sherman Crunchley was a police officer.

His great-great-great (you get the idea) grandfather was the first ever chief of police in Biscuit City. A Crunchley had been the chief of police ever since, including Sherman's great-grandmother, Weezelda Crunchley. Kirby Crunchley, Sherman's father, was the current chief. In a month, when his father retired, Sherman was in line to take his place.

But Sherman hated being a police officer. He only did it because
it was expected of him.

Sherman's problem was that he was too nice. He couldn't bear to
say no to anyone or anything.

When someone pleaded, "Please don't give me a parking ticket,"
he would say, "Well, okay!" and look the other way.

If he had to break up a fight, he would run in with a box of doughnuts and yell, "FREE SNACKS!" to distract everyone.

He ended up doing all the boring paperwork at the office because he was the only one who never said no to the sergeant.

Sherman really didn't enjoy anything about his job—except maybe the hat.

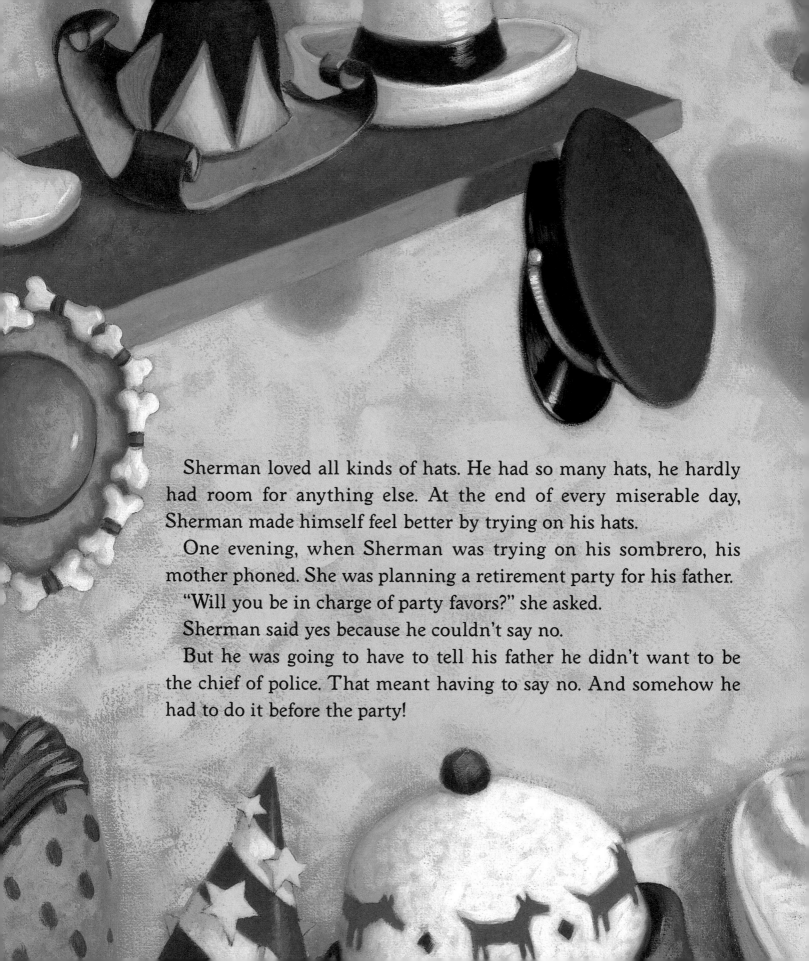

Sherman loved all kinds of hats. He had so many hats, he hardly had room for anything else. At the end of every miserable day, Sherman made himself feel better by trying on his hats.

One evening, when Sherman was trying on his sombrero, his mother phoned. She was planning a retirement party for his father.

"Will you be in charge of party favors?" she asked.

Sherman said yes because he couldn't say no.

But he was going to have to tell his father he didn't want to be the chief of police. That meant having to say no. And somehow he had to do it before the party!

He decided to go to the library for help. Sherman found the perfect book: *How to Say No.*

When he got home, Sherman realized it was a book about how to say no in foreign languages.

He read it anyway. By the time he'd finished it, he could say no in Japanese, Spanish, French, and several languages he'd never even heard of.

But he still couldn't say no to his father.

That night Sherman couldn't sleep. While he was watching "The Late, Late, Late [you get the idea] Show," he saw a commercial. It was for a video called *Must Say No*. He ordered it, with special "next day" delivery.

When it arrived, Sherman ripped open the box. The video was
How to Raise Snails. They had sent him the wrong tape!

He called the number on the box to complain. A nice lady
answered. "Hello," she said. "Were you pleased with the tape, sir?"

Sherman said yes and hung up.

The party was coming up soon, and Sherman was growing more and more upset. When Sherman got upset, he liked to buy a new hat. He looked through the newspaper to see if there were any hats on sale. On the last page, he saw an ad that made him very excited.

WANT TO LOSE WEIGHT?
ARE YOU AFRAID OF THE DARK?
SEE ME—PROFESSOR HAMBONI—
WORLD'S GREATEST HYPNOTIST!

That was it! If Sherman got hypnotized, he'd be able to tell his father!

Sherman called Professor Hamboni. The professor told him to come over right away.

When he knocked on Professor Hamboni's door, a small dog wearing a big turban answered.

"Nice hat," said Sherman. Then he told Hamboni his problem.

"I can help you!" said Professor Hamboni. He sat Sherman down in a chair and swung a golden dog tag slowly in front of Sherman's eyes. "You are getting sleepy," he said.

Sherman fell asleep immediately.

"When you wake up, you will say, 'No, I don't want to be the chief of police!'" Professor Hamboni told Sherman. Then he tapped Sherman on the shoulder.

Sherman woke up. "I don't want to be the thief of the fleas!" he said.

The professor tried again.

When Sherman woke up, he said, "I don't want to be the chief of slow geese!"

"One more time," said Professor Hamboni, bringing out his special crystal.

This time Sherman said, "I don't want to be the beef or the cheese!"

"I give up!" said Professor Hamboni.

Sherman gave up, too. It looked as if he was going to be Biscuit City's next chief of police after all.

At home, there was a message from his mother reminding him that the party was in two days. Sherman sighed and got to work on the party favors. He had decided to make everyone a different kind of hat. Even though he had fun creating them, Sherman was heartbroken.

Then, as he was decorating a hat, he had an idea—a wild and crazy idea. But could he do it? Would he be able to pull it off?

The night of the party, Sherman was really nervous. He watched while everyone danced and admired one another's party hats.

Finally it was time for Sherman's father to pass the Biscuit City chief of police badge on to his son.

Sherman's mother said, "Please find your seat by looking at the place cards Sherman made."

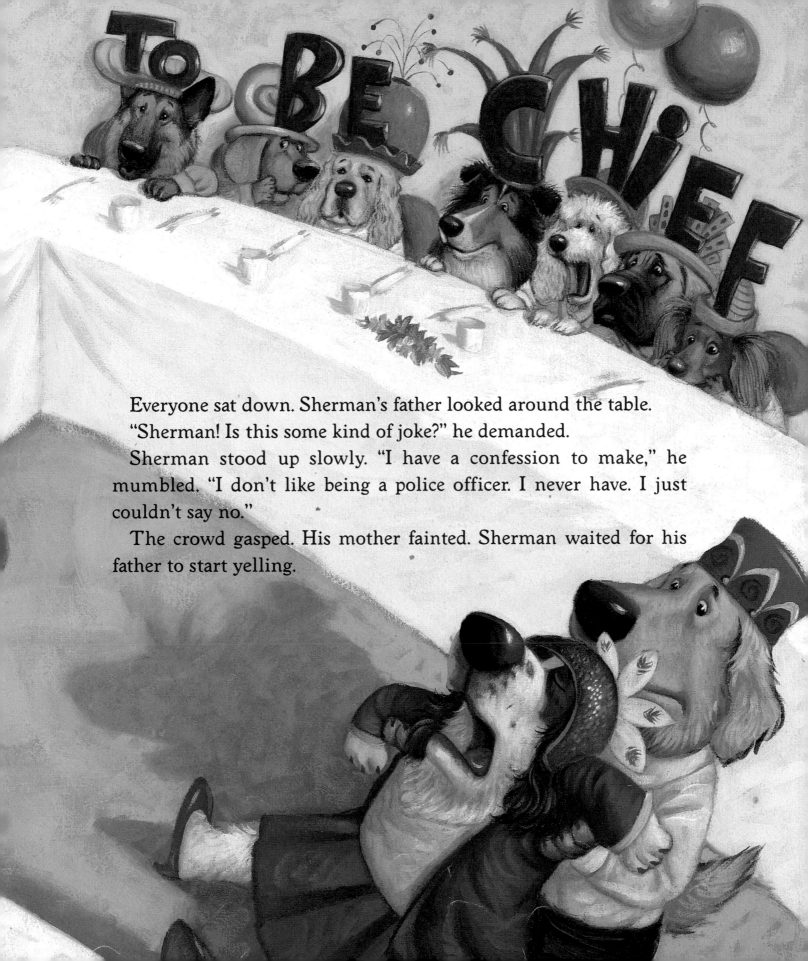

Everyone sat down. Sherman's father looked around the table.
"Sherman! Is this some kind of joke?" he demanded.

Sherman stood up slowly. "I have a confession to make," he mumbled. "I don't like being a police officer. I never have. I just couldn't say no."

The crowd gasped. His mother fainted. Sherman waited for his father to start yelling.

But his father began laughing instead. He laughed and laughed and . . . well, you get the idea!

"I have a confession, too, son," his father said. "I don't really want to retire. I was only doing it because I thought you wanted to be the chief of police. And how could I say no to you?"

Sherman heaved a big sigh of relief.

"I guess you're the new old chief of police," he said.

"Hip hip hooray!" cousin Dudley shouted. Everyone cheered, including Sherman's mother.

"Would you like a job in the cafeteria?" his father asked.

Sherman thought for a second. "No, thank you!" he answered.

"Well said!" his father replied.

"Then what *are* you going to do, Sherman?" his mother asked.

"Oh, I'm sure I'll figure something out. . . ." said Sherman.